sleepover Girls

Sleepover Girls is published by Capstone Young Readers
A Capstone Imprint
1710 Roe Crest Drive, North Mankato, Minnesota 56003
www.capstoneyoungreaders.com

Copyright © 2016 by Capstone Young Readers

Library of Congress Cataloging-in-Publication data is
available on the Library of Congress website.
ISBN: 978-1-62370-306-6 (paperback)
ISBN: 978-1-4965-0543-9 (library binding)
ISBN: 978-1-62370-578-7 (eBook)
ISBN: 978-1-4965-2352-5 (eBook PDF)

Summary: Anyone who knows Ashley knows she is super serious
about her blog, Magstar, and now she has taken it up a notch with
her new YouTube channel! Making the fashion and beauty videos is a
total blast, and when one of her videos gets featured on a major teen
mag website, she goes from amateur to overnight online celeb.
Suddenly all of the older girls at school want to be her BFF.
But with everything going on, can she still find time to juggle
school, family, and most of all, the Sleepover Girls?

Designed by Alison Thiele

Illustrated by Paula Franco

Printed in the United States of America in Stevens Point, Wisconsin.
052015   008824WZF15

sleepover Girls

Ashley
Goes
VIRAL

by Jen Jones

CAPSTONE YOUNG READERS
a capstone imprint

Maren Melissa Taylor

Maren is what you'd call "personality-plus" — sassy, bursting with energy, and always ready with a sharp one-liner. She dreams of becoming an actress or comedienne one day and moving to Hollywood to make it big. Not one to fuss over fashion, you'll often catch Maren wearing a hoodie over a sports tee and jeans. She is an only child, so she has adopted her friends as sisters.

Willow Marie Keys

Patient and kind, Willow is a wonderful
confidante and friend. (Just ask her twin,
Winston!) She is also a budding artist with
creativity for miles. She will definitely own
her own store one day, selling everything she
makes. Growing up in a hippie-esque family,
Willow acquired a Bohemian style that
perfectly suits her flower child within.

Delaney Ann Brand

Delaney's smart and motivated — and she's always on the go! Whether she's volunteering at the animal shelter or helping Maren with her homework, you can always count on Delaney. You'll usually spot low-maintenance Delaney in a ponytail and jeans (and don't forget her special charm bracelet, with unique charms to symbolize each one of the Sleepover Girls). She is a great role model for her younger sister, Gigi.

Ashley Francesca Maggio

Ashley is the baby of a lively Italian family.
Her older siblings (Josie, Roman, Gino, and Matt)
have taught her a lot, including how to get
attention in such a big family, which Ashley has
become a pro at. This fashionista-turned-blogger
is on top of every style trend and shares it with
the world via her blog, Magstar. Vivacious and
mischievous, Ashley is rarely sighted without
her beloved "purse puppy," Coco.

chapter One

As the limo neared the red carpet, I could see blinding flashes of light popping all around. Paparazzi and private cars were everywhere. Was this really my life now? And, oh my, was that one of the *Project Runway* judges? I couldn't help but have a moment as I peeked through the window at the glamorous scene unfolding before me.

"Wait, let's do a touch-up before you step out of the car," insisted my makeup artist, Fiona. She was always at the ready with a dab of gloss or puff of powder.

I obediently pouted my lips as she put on one more coat of lipstick to finish off my look. She handed me a mirror so I could check out the total effect — not bad! One of my favorite designers, Sirena Simons, had sent over a handmade party dress designed especially for me, and I absolutely loved it. It was a gorgeous royal purple and had poufy short sleeves and an adorable bubble-style skirt. It was fun, frilly, and fab. If there was ever a dress that fit my personality, this was it!

"Ready?" asked my publicist, leaning over to open the door. I nodded that I was. "You're going to kill it on the carpet!" My dog, Coco, let out a little bark, as if to say she agreed.

The minute I stepped onto the red carpet, I was swept up into a whirlwind of people, lights, and pure chaos. I loved it! I barely had time to snap a selfie of me and Coco before a little girl sitting in the bleachers screamed and pointed at us. "Ashley! Ashley! Can I have your autograph? Please?"

I whipped out my Sharpie in record time. "Of course!" I said, scrawling my autograph and finishing it with a star. I tried to stand there and talk to my fan, but before I could get a conversation going, my publicist grabbed my arm and ushered me over to the booth of the top entertainment show on TV.

I tried not to get nervous as I stared at the "On-Air" sign flashing above the host's head.

"Ashley Maggio, hi!" the host exclaimed loudly, squinting a little to read her cue cards better. "You're one of the blogosphere's hottest stars right now. What made you decide to start your blog, Magstar?"

I relaxed a little as the host thrust the microphone in my face. After all, I could talk about my blog all day! "Well, I started Magstar a few years ago as a way to further explore my passion for fashion," I replied, looking straight into the camera. "Now it's become practically a full-time job, between my YouTube channel, all the social media stuff, and — of course — the blog!"

The host flashed her mega-watt grin at me. "Well, I'd say that's pretty impressive for anyone, let alone a sixth grader," she said, nodding in approval. "I think you've got a bright future ahead of you, Ms. Maggio."

I smiled right back and put on my designer sunglasses jokingly. "Well, I guess I'd better wear shades, then!" I waved at the camera and stepped back onto the red carpet, where I was greeted with shouts of "Ashley! Ashley! Ashley!" from the crowd in the bleachers. It was truly a pinch-me kind of moment.

The shouts seemed to be getting louder and louder, until it almost felt like they were screaming right in my ear. "ASHLEY! ASHLEY!"

I sat up with a jolt, only to see my three besties leaning over me. Suddenly I was transported off the red carpet and onto my friend Maren's couch. I blinked, struggling to make sense of what was happening. The girls all dissolved into laughter after seeing how out of it I was. "What's going on?" I stammered, trying to get out of my daze.

"Let's just say you fell asleep pretty much right after the opening credits finished rolling," said Delaney, waving the DVD cover in the air. "We've been yelling your name for the last five minutes."

So much for watching a chick flick! Usually I was glued to the screen.

"OMG," I said, laughing right along with them. "I guess that's what I get for staying up until all hours last night updating my profile page for the *Stylish Tween* contest. But it's just such an amazing opportunity!" I was super pumped — our favorite mag was holding a contest to find its "Top Fashion Blogger." The prize? A $500 shopping spree and a chance to be featured on the *Stylish Tween* website with a "Day in the Life" video. Sweet!

Maren grinned. She and the other girls were used to me always doing one crazy thing or another for my blog. "Ahhh, so that's why you turned into Sleeping Beauty," she said. "Now it all makes sense."

I reached for a sip of sparkling water, hoping it would pep me up a bit. Even if winning the contest would be worth it, falling asleep early at a sleepover was really bad form!

"You guys, I had the craziest dream," I told them. "I dreamed that my blog had made me famous and that I was at this fabulous red carpet event dressed in a Sirena Simons original."

Willow giggled and handed me a plate of chocolate-covered pretzels.

"The dream isn't all that far from reality," she said. "I checked out your new YouTube channel the other day, and your videos all had tons of views! My guess is you've got this *Stylish Tween* thing in the bag."

"Oh, please," I told her. "I'm far from the most talented person in this room, let alone on the whole Internet."

And it was true. My BFFs were all totally talented in their own ways. The only thing wilder than Maren's sense of humor was her curly, fire-red hair. I was positive that one day we'd see her name in lights as one of the country's top comediennes. Delaney was the brainiac of the bunch, and she had the straight-A record to show for it. As for Willow, the girl was a true DIY goddess, from crafting, to art projects, to upcycling furniture. (I was hoping she'd help me make some cool pieces to create a set for my future fashion videos.)

I guess we were all kind of rock stars in our own rights. Maybe that's why we were such good friends. Our tradition of holding sleepovers every Friday had earned us the nickname the Sleepover Girls at school.

I didn't want to take over the whole convo by talking about my blog, so I changed the subject. "It's not even midnight yet!" I exclaimed. "I know what'll get me my second wind — a good, old-fashioned round of karaoke. Who's down?"

Delaney nodded in excitement, but Willow looked iffy. She wasn't exactly the most outgoing person on the planet, even when it was just the four of us. Luckily for her, Maren wasn't feeling the idea either. "Love the idea, but my mom will not be impressed if we wake up the terrible twosome," she said, frowning.

Maren's mom had recently gotten remarried, and her new stepsiblings, Alice and Ace (twins!), stayed with her family every other weekend. It hadn't been the easiest adjustment for Maren to make, but she was coming around slowly but surely. It was all about baby steps, right?

Willow reached into her bag and pulled out her nail art kit. "I've got the second-best thing," she said, dangling a neon pink polish in the air. "Manis for everyone! I brought nail bling."

We were all on board with that idea. After all, Willow was a whiz at nail art (and pretty much every other kind of art, too). As we started getting pretty, I felt my second wind coming on. Being around my friends was just the energy boost this girl needed.

chapter Two

"Thanks for the ride, Mrs. Brand!" I yelled to Delaney's mom as she pulled out of my driveway. Sleepover number 37,248 (not really, but it did feel like we'd been doing it forever) was officially *finito*. I was already counting the minutes until next Friday! I guess you could call me completely sleepover obsessed. Luckily, I'd get more BFF time tomorrow, when Delaney, Maren, and Willow would be coming over to help me shoot a new video for my blog.

"Incoming!" yelled my brother Roman, who was sitting on our porch with my other brothers Gino and Matt.

Suddenly, I heard a loud noise and a remote control helicopter whizzed within inches of my nose! I immediately ducked down to the ground. My brothers doubled over laughing at my dramatic reaction as the toy helicopter continued flying wildly around. There was never a dull moment in the Maggio household.

Annoyed, I ran over to swat Roman on the arm. "Are you trying to kill me?" I huffed. "Your pilot skills could use a little work."

I grabbed the remote from him and started flying the helicopter around myself, landing it on the sidewalk. "There. Grounded, like you should be after your attempt to kill me."

"Talk about being dramatic," said Roman, snatching the remote back from me. "It was just a joke."

"Here's an idea," Gino said. "How about you go inside and play with your toys while we play with ours? They sure take up enough room in the basement."

My parents had recently helped me set up a dedicated filming area in the basement, with a really cool backdrop and lighting to help make my videos look more professional. Of course, my brothers weren't overly excited about that, since the basement doubled as our "fun room." There was a big-screen TV, vintage pinball games, and even an old jukebox. Needless to say, there was never a shortage of things to do during sleepovers at my house!

"It looked like you guys had plenty of room to lounge around when you spent all of last weekend on the couch, hogging the TV and watching ESPN non-stop," I complained.

Before they could respond, I headed into the house and slammed the door behind me.

These were the moments when I really missed my sister, Josie, who was off at college. Fending off three older brothers could be exhausting! Luckily, I carried the girl-power torch well, even without Josie around to back me up.

"Hey! The Trailblazers were playing. What did you expect?" Roman called after me. I heard them laugh again as the helicopter started buzzing in the air. For high school boys, they definitely weren't as mature as you would expect. No wonder they mostly hung out with each other instead of girls their age!

My mood improved considerably when I went into my bedroom and saw my mom just starting to put a giant box on my bed. "You've got mail!" she chirped.

I leaped onto the bed and tore open the box. "What. Is. THIS?" I exclaimed. Inside were ten different pairs of shoes. I dangled a pair of silver kitten heels in the air with glee. "Did Style

Santa come early? Because this feels a whole lot like Christmas!"

My mom pulled out a letter from the box and read it over. "Stepz Shoes loves your blog and they want you to do a series of videos about their new collection," she said excitedly. "In return, they'll send you a box of shoes every month for three months, plus two thousand dollars!"

My jaw dropped. I'd heard about some of the other young fashion bloggers getting endorsement deals and free swag, but I didn't think I'd quite reached that level yet.

"Let me process this," I said. "I'm getting paid to talk about shoes? That would be a big, fat YES! Do you know how many Sirena Simons bags I could buy with that money? All of my dreams are coming true!"

My mom wasn't having that. "Slow down, sweetie. You could buy a lot of things, but there are a lot of better uses for the money," she said.

"And that's exactly why your dad and I will handle the money if you decide to do this. That will help your college fund quite nicely!"

I gave her an "Are you serious?" look. "Well, that's lame," I said, only half-kidding.

But I knew it was part of the deal. My mom and dad had made me promise to give them access to my email account and all the other blog stuff. They didn't want any shady people trying to take advantage of me. Plus, I knew they had my best interests at heart — I hoped to study fashion design at school one day. And saving this money would definitely help me afford it.

My mom handed me a pair of adorable tan wedges. "I think the monthly shoe delivery will more than make up for it," she said. And I had to agree! I couldn't wait to tell the girls about my shoe-filled surprise.

As if on cue, my phone rang. I eagerly grabbed it, hoping it was one of the Sleepover

Girls. But a picture of my friend Sophie flashed up on the screen instead. I debated whether to answer; she and I hadn't really been on great terms since the bully incident.

In short, here's the backstory: Delaney had led a big anti-cyberbullying campaign for student council, and in the process, busted Sophie for doing just that to one of our classmates.

Sophie had since apologized to everyone (including Marcie, the girl she bullied), but things hadn't really been the same. She and I had gone from hanging out all the time to pretty much only seeing each other in science class (where we were lab partners).

Though I'd been a little sad to spend less time with my new friend, I was really disappointed in her, too. But I was dying to tell someone my news, and Sophie of all people would get it. She was probably the only person in our class who freaked out about fashion as much as me.

"Soph?" I answered. My mom smiled and snuck out of the room.

Sophie sounded kind of surprised that I'd picked up. "Oh, hey, Ash!" she said. "I just left the mall and I was missing you, so I thought I'd see what's up in your world."

A grin spread over my face. "Well, you might want to Facetime me to find out," I told her. "Some things are just better shared visually."

We connected on Facetime, and I dumped the box out onto the bed, panning the screen across all of the shoes. "Guess who just got an endorsement deal with Stepz Shoes?"

Sophie looked shocked. "Shut the front door!" she screamed. "No way. I love Stepz stuff!"

I beamed and told her all of the delicious details. It felt good to reconnect with her, even if it was over something as silly as shoes.

"So are you going to do it?" she asked. "I'm guessing that's not even a question."

I flopped back onto the bed and snuggled up with my fuzzy pink pillow. "Totally!" I answered. "I can't wait to get started. I already have my video all planned out for tomorrow, but maybe I can do Stepz for the next one."

Sophie's eyes lit up. "Did someone say video shoot tomorrow?" she asked. "Count me in. It's been forever since we did one of your shoots."

I squirmed uncomfortably. "Well, Willow, Ashley, and Delaney are already helping me," I said. "Not to turn you down, but it might be better to give them a little more breathing room."

"Point taken," said Sophie, looking bummed. "Maybe I could still come over this week and see the shoes in person? It'd be fun to hang out."

Now that I could do. I didn't want things to be weird anymore, and everyone deserved a second chance, right?

"Consider it a date!" I told her.

chapter Three

"Be careful up there!" shouted Delaney. She was holding the stepladder on which Maren was precariously perched. Maren was using clothespins to hang the hot pink sheet that would be the video's backdrop, but watching her teeter was a bit scary. She was known for being on the clumsy side.

"Yeah, I need all of my co-stars in one piece, please," I joked.

I loved the fact that I actually had co-stars for once. Usually I was riding solo in my blog posts and videos, but every once in a while, my dog Coco made an appearance. (After all, she was my favorite accessory!) Sophie had also been in a few of my photo shoots before all the drama happened with Marcie. I was pumped that the Sleepover Girls would be taking the spotlight this time!

We all held our breath as Maren leaned over on one foot to finish the job. "Dunzo!" she proclaimed proudly, climbing down to everyone's relief.

Willow looked up from the heart decoration she was cutting. "Looks awesome!" she said, giving an enthusiastic thumbs-up. She'd helped me design a lot of my sets in the past, so I was glad the backdrop got her seal of approval.

I rubbed my hands together in excitement. "Okay, it's almost go time!" I exclaimed. "Let's do a quick outfit check and then we'll get started."

I led the girls over to the clothing rack, where I'd hung up a suggested look for each of them. Since Valentine's Day was coming up, I'd decided to do a "V-Day Looks We Heart" video, in which we'd all model different styles. I'd picked every outfit specially to go with each girl's personality.

Delaney was up first. She was the definition of "casual cutie" and regularly rocked the simple ponytail and jeans look. Being so busy with student council and soccer, she barely had time to get dressed in the morning, let alone care what she was wearing. I handed her the outfit I'd selected, which was a thin gray sweatshirt with a giant heart on the front and red jeans. "What do you think?" Delaney asked, holding it up in front of her.

"Looking good!" said Maren. "Whatcha got for me, Ash?" Maren's closet was mostly full of sports jerseys and sweatpants, so she was a little harder to dress. I'd found the perfect thing for her, but first I had a little trick up my sleeve.

I held up a frilly, flowered dress that looked like something Laura Ingalls might wear, paired with a giant hair bow. "I thought the bow would pair really nicely with your red hair," I told her, playing dumb. "Ginger-rific!"

Maren touched the dress like it was a hot potato. The word girly wasn't in her vocabulary. "The things I do for you, Ash," she grumbled. "But I guess I'll try it on."

That was one of the things we all loved about Maren — she was always willing to try anything! Luckily for her, I was totally kidding. "Did you seriously think I would make you wear that?" I said, grabbing her real outfit. It was a dress made out of a sports jersey that said "#1 Heartbreaker."

Maren let out a deep breath, while Delaney and Willow giggled at my switcheroo. "Phew!"

she said, looking the dress over with approval. "For a hot minute, I thought I was getting the makeover of a lifetime."

"That's what I'm here for — to expand your horizons," I joked. "And speaking of horizons, I've got a super-earthy, bohemian look for our sunshine girl Willow."

I opened up a box to reveal a gorgeous flower crown I'd bought especially for the shoot. They were all the rage at the big music festivals, and I'd been dying to feature one on Magstar. Plus, I knew the look would be just right for hippie chick Willow, especially with the sundress I'd picked out.

"No way!" she exclaimed, taking the crown out of the box to admire it. "I've always wanted to make one of these."

Maren bent over to take a whiff. "Mmmm," she said, savoring the flowery smell. "You gotta stop and smell the roses every once in a while.

Just as long as they're not on a dress." She shot me a fake stern look.

"So true," said Delaney, taking a little whiff of her own. "Now let's get to business!"

Delaney's bossiness definitely came in handy sometimes. The girls went to get changed while I double-checked the camera settings and the tripod height. Everything looked good, so I decided it was time to get into my own outfit: a coral-colored, fit-and-flare dress with a pleated bottom. It was the perfect date look . . . for people who actually *had* dates. (My parents said I was too young to date, but that didn't stop me from having a major crush on Grant Thompson.)

I quickly forgot all about Grant as Delaney, Willow, and Maren came strutting back down the steps.

"Well, if it isn't the Valentine's Day vixens," I joked. "You guys look amazing!"

Maren struck a supermodel pose. "We know how to work it," she said, laughing as Willow took up a similar pose beside her.

Delaney giggled. "Save it for the camera, ladies! We've got a run-through to do." Again, bless Delaney for being bossy. I could always count on her to do my dirty work for me.

The run-through basically just consisted of me practicing my opening talk and then inviting each of the girls, one by one, to show off their looks. I also showed everyone how to work the camera, since we were going to take turns running it. Everything went perfectly, so it was finally time for the real thing!

"Delaney, I'm surprised you didn't bring a director's slate," I joked, taking a seat on my bench in front of the camera. "I know how much you like to call the shots."

She giggled. "Who needs a slate when you've got a loud mouth?" she said. "ACTION!"

Willow clicked "Record," and I launched into my monologue. "Hi! I'm Ashley, and welcome to the Magstar YouTube channel," I said brightly. "If you're here for fierce fashion and all the style news fit to print, you've come to the right place! Today we're going to be focusing on Looks We Heart in honor of V-Day, of course. What will you be wearing on February fourteenth? Whether you're coupled up or single and mingling, I've got some great suggestions, and we're going to model them for you right now. Meet my sweethearts — the Sleepover Girls!"

I motioned to Delaney to join me in front of the camera and started to launch into her introduction, but before she could walk out, a loud buzzing sound started drowning me out. "What is that?" I said, wondering if the camera had started to break. All of a sudden, a toy helicopter flew right through my shot! The girls started screaming as it flew wildly around the room.

"You GUYS!" I yelled, knowing my brothers couldn't be far away. Sure enough, Gino, Matt, and Roman stood at the top of the steps, laughing uncontrollably. "Gotcha!" said Roman. "Bet that video will get a lot of views."

Maren, Willow, and Delaney started laughing along with them, but I just folded my arms. "Way to ruin the shot, guys," I said.

"Oh, c'mon, Ash, you have to admit it's a little funny," said Maren. "It's not every day that you get photo-bombed by a toy helicopter."

I let a little smile creep out, but I was still annoyed. There was so much to do, and I still had to edit the video after everyone left. "I guess," I said, unconvinced. I turned back to my brothers. "When are you guys going to grow up?"

I already knew the answer to that: never! At least I knew my besties would be on my side, no matter what. That always made me feel better.

chapter Four

The next morning, I rolled over to press the snooze button yet again, hoping for just a few more precious minutes of sleep. I managed to barely get my eyes open enough to see the time: 7:49?! I was supposed to be at school in twenty minutes. Oh no! I never overslept. How many times had I pressed snooze? Time to get ready at warp speed!

I was throwing on my robe to hop into the shower when I heard a loud knock on the door. "Yo, Ash! Ready to take off?" asked Gino, peeking his head in. He drove me to school sometimes when my parents had to leave early for work. (And we were lucky to make it there, as it was always an adventure driving around in Gino's beat-up car.)

"Does it look like it?" I said, gesturing to my robe. "I'm freaking out! Why didn't you guys wake me up?"

Gino shrugged. "I thought you'd been getting ready this whole time. It's not like you've never been holed up in your room putting on makeup and picking out clothes before."

He did have a point. "Can you give me five minutes to take a speed shower?" I pleaded. "I really can't be late today."

"Sure," said Gino. "Meet me downstairs in five." He took a bite of his power bar and disappeared down the steps without a care in the world.

In record time, I managed to fly through the shower, throw on some clothes, and get all of my stuff for school into my bag. Once I was safely buckled in Gino's car, I shut my eyes for a second to try to chill out a bit. Whew! That was a close call. I guess I shouldn't have stayed up so late trying to edit the video we'd shot last night.

"Have a good day at school, dear," called Gino in a fake mom voice as he dropped me off at the entrance to Valley View Middle School. I gave a quick wave, then sprinted off toward the doors. Somehow I managed to sneak into homeroom and into my seat just in time.

Our teacher had barely started talking when I felt a tap on my shoulder. "Ashley, your sweater is on inside out," whispered Marcie, who was sitting nearby.

So much for being a glam girl 24/7. Today I felt more like a disheveled diva. Schoolgirl by day, Magstar by night, and utterly tired in between.

I flashed her a grateful smile. "Thanks, Marcie!" I whispered. I grabbed the scarf I was wearing as a hair accessory and put it around my neck instead, hoping it would cover up the tag. As soon as the bell rang, I shot out of my seat so I could go fix myself in the bathroom.

"Hey, girl," came Delaney's familiar voice from down the hallway. "Wait up!"

She caught up with me and linked arms. "We missed you this morning before school," she said. "How did the video editing go last night?"

I groaned. "It took forever, and I ended up oversleeping," I said. "Hence the hot mess of an outfit."

Delaney took a minute to give me the once-over. "Oh, wow," she said, taking a lock of my hair in her hand. "I don't think I've ever seen you come to school with wet hair! And the ensemble is definitely not what we're used to seeing from our resident fashionista. But who cares? Even soggy, you still look great. Plus, I've got some news that will make your bad day a whole lot better."

I grabbed her hand and dragged her toward the bathroom with me. "Tell me in here," I urged. "We only have a few minutes until next period and I've got to at least get my sweater right side out! I owe my Magstar readers that much," I joked.

Once we were safely in the bathroom, Delaney hopped up on the counter excitedly. "Soooo . . ." she began. "I was browsing the *Stylish Tween* website this morning, and guess what? You're one of the top ten semi-finalists for Top Fashion Blogger!"

I gasped. "No. Way!" I exclaimed. I'd been in such a rush this morning I hadn't even thought to check. Again, thank heavens for Delaney!

Delaney whipped out her phone to show me the announcement. There it was: my picture, a little description of my blog, links to my Instagram and Twitter, and a list of the other nine semi-finalists. Woo-hoo! I couldn't wait to check my email and find out what came next.

"Have I told you lately that I heart you?" I said, giving her a hug. Delaney didn't really care about fashion, but she cared about me — and that mattered a lot.

Our warm fuzzies were interrupted when one of the bathroom stall doors opened and Kate Homan came out. She was a seventh grader whom Sophie hung out with a lot, and not necessarily the nicest person on the planet. "Cute look, Ashley," said Kate, her tone suggesting she thought the exact opposite. "You might want to step it up a little bit if you want to win the competition. Ta-ta! Got to get to class now."

She flounced away, and Delaney rolled her eyes. She was no fan of Kate's, especially since Kate had been one of the cyberbullies who had picked on Marcie. "Typical. But she was right about one thing — we do need to hurry up and get to class. See you at lunch!" Delaney bolted out the door, never one to be late to anything.

Even though there were only a few minutes left before class, I couldn't resist checking my inbox on my phone, and sure enough, there was an email from *Stylish Tween*. It said:

Dear Ashley,

Congratulations on being one of our top ten semi-finalists for Stylish Tween's *Top Fashion Blogger! Soon we are going to be narrowing down the voting pool to just the top five, and we'd like you to fill out the attached form so we can update your profile. Tell us what you'd include in your Day in the Life video, and we'll have our readers vote on which blogger they want to see! Please return the form no later than next Wednesday. Good luck!*

I squealed and skipped out the door. Today was definitely turning around!

I managed to make it through English, history, and study hall without any more fashion police commentary on my very un-Ashley outfit. By the time I made it to the caf for lunch, I was feeling great, despite the day's frantic start. I started heading straight for our table, but Sophie intercepted me before I could sit down with the Sleepover Girls.

"Ash, come here for a minute," called Sophie, who was sitting with Kate and some of the other seventh graders. She pretty much only hung out with the older crowd now. "Kate told us all about the *Stylish Tween* contest! You go, girl."

So Kate *wasn't* too cool for little old me after all — she'd taken the time to spread the word to her loyal flock. But, in this case, it might have been a blessing. I needed all the votes I could get! "It's true," I told her. "I just found out I'm in the top ten. I have to submit a sample itinerary for a 'Day in the Life' video in case I make the top five."

Kate looked directly at me, taking a bite of a carrot stick. "So, if you win, can we be in your video?" she asked. "I'm sure you'd love to have some of the most fashionable people at VVMS to show off."

Kate and her buddies wouldn't normally be at the top of my list, but I didn't want to be rude. Plus, what were the chances I was really going to win this thing, anyway? "Sure, why not?" I said. "But only if you vote for me every day!"

"Count on it," said Sophie. She gave me a little wink, and I smiled back. I wasn't about to fall under Kate's spell, but maybe it was about time Sophie and I started getting back on track!

chapter Five

And that's exactly what Sophie and I did. Later that week in science class, we got to be lab partners for yet another of Mr. Tanner's brilliant biology assignments. He loved to assign hands-on projects, which usually resulted in us doing random stuff like making a potato-powered clock. Today we were going to make edible cells. And rather than dreading another overly polite, strained science class with Sophie, I was actually kind of looking forward to working with her today.

"Is it just me, or are you getting hungry too?" whispered Sophie as she eyed the materials Mr. Tanner had set out on our table. There were graham crackers, M&M's, Twizzlers, Nilla Wafers, and other goodies. By the looks of it, this was going to be a lot more fun than dissecting a frog (which we'd done not too long ago).

"I might eat our project before Mr. Tanner has time to grade it," I whispered back, dangling a Twizzler in front of my face. "You don't care if we get an F, right?"

"An F never tasted so good," said Sophie, stuffing an M&M in her mouth before Mr. Tanner could see.

Mr. Tanner clapped his hands together to get the class's attention. "Okay, so I've written which foods go with certain cell parts," he said, hitting the white board with a pointer. "For instance, the Nilla Wafers act as the nucleus, while the Twizzlers form the cell wall, the frosting forms the cytoplasm, and so on. Your job is to recreate what a plant cell looks like with these foods, using the diagram I've provided. Get to it!"

He turned on some classical music, probably to inspire us while we made our edible plant cells. Out of the corner of my eye, I could see Delaney and Marcie starting to put their project together. I tried to shake off the feeling that I was doing something wrong by being all buddy-buddy with Sophie again. After all, there was no sense dwelling on the past, right?

All of a sudden, a Nilla Wafer flew Frisbee-style onto our table. I whipped around to see who'd thrown it and then blushed when I found out. It was Grant Thompson! He was forever torturing me and Sophie in science class, but secretly I didn't mind. I'd take any attention from Grant I could get! I self-consciously smoothed my blue skirt and sent him a flirty smile to let him know it didn't faze me.

Sophie wasn't quite so forgiving. She immediately grabbed the tube of white frosting and used it to write "Grow up" on one of the graham crackers. After waiting until Mr. Tanner's head was down, she turned toward Grant and held the graham cracker up to her forehead.

He responded by lobbing another Nilla Wafer at us, which Sophie promptly threw right back at him. I covered my mouth to stifle a giggle that was threatening to escape. From across the room, Delaney was watching the whole exchange curiously. And it turned out Mr. Tanner was watching, too.

"Sophie, Grant, and Ashley, could you come up here for a moment?" said Mr. Tanner, sounding frustrated.

As we approached Mr. Tanner's desk, my stomach did a little flip. I hoped he wouldn't give us a zero on the assignment. I'd been a little behind on my schoolwork lately, since I'd been devoting most of my attention to Magstar. A glaring F definitely wouldn't help matters (even if it did taste good)!

"Mr. Thompson, does this look like the cafeteria?" asked Mr. Tanner.

"Um, no, sir," answered Grant, putting on his best "I'm sorry" face. He looked down to avoid my and Sophie's gaze.

"Then there's no reason to start a food fight, is there?" said Mr. Tanner. "And as for you, Sophie, I would think you would have learned your lesson about being nice to others in this class." So he had seen everything. Did teachers have eyes on the backs of their heads or something? Impressive.

Sophie nodded but didn't say anything. Mr. Tanner continued, "Now, get to work, and I don't want any more interruptions or I'll be forced to send all three of you to detention." He waved his hand as if to say he was done with us.

We trudged back to our seats obediently, and I picked up the diagram so we could catch up with everyone else.

"I guess we'd better get serious," I told Sophie, hoping she'd be okay with buckling down.

"Don't worry. We'll get it done. But let's get together after school. After all, I still have to check out those gorgeous Stepz Shoes. We can have fun without having to worry about Mr. Wizard or Grant," she said.

I pretended to be writing something down so Mr. Tanner wouldn't see us talking. "Okay, you can come over, but I'm shooting a video today," I whispered. "Wanna help?"

"Is the sky blue? Is Sirena Simons a fashion goddess?" Sophie said. "Of course! I'm so in."

"Awesome," I told her. "Now, help me figure out where to put these green M&M's."

We put our heads together and managed to finish our edible plant cell in the nick of time.

Sophie raised her hand to signal that we were done, and Mr. Tanner came over to give it a look. "Now that's more like it, girls," he said. "See what happens when you get down to business? You can go ahead and eat your cells now."

Sophie and I held up our graham crackers and did a fake toast. I caught Delaney's eye again and smiled brightly at her, but she just turned away. She was lab partners with Marcie, who was certainly no fan of Sophie's (not that I blamed her). I tried to catch up with Delaney when the bell rang, but she'd already hightailed it out of the classroom.

"See you at Casa Maggio later!" called Sophie, heading off to her next class. She definitely had more pep in her step now that we were on talking terms again.

chapter Six

Just like old times, it was really fun having Sophie along for the video shoot later that day. I'd forgotten just how much her creative spark really helped light my own fashionista fire!

"Check this out," said Sophie, who was cozied up on my sofa while she looked up YouTube videos on her phone. "I found this old eighties movie trailer, where all they show in the frame are different feet dancing to the same song.

That could be a really cute way to introduce each of the Stepz styles!"

After watching the clip, I could see exactly what Sophie was talking about. It would be a super fun, upbeat way to show off all the shoes. "Perfect!" I told her. "Love it. Maybe we could take turns wearing each of the shoes and dancing in them for the video."

"Totally," she said, grabbing a pair of wedge sandals. "But let me see if they fit. I think I wear a bigger size than you." Sophie slipped on the sandal, and it fit just like a glove. "It's my Cinderella moment." She giggled. "It may not be a glass slipper, but it's the perfect fit."

And laughing along with her, I was starting to remember just how much our friendship was the perfect fit, too. Two stylish tweens, reunited at last!

As it turned out, word spread quickly about me and Sophie making nice. Walking up the pathway to school Thursday morning, I was met by an enthusiastic Kate Homan. Say *what*? I was pretty sure she hadn't known my name until a few days ago.

"Morning, Ashley!" she said, holding the door open for me. "Sophie told me your video shoot yesterday was an absolute blast."

We fell into step together walking toward the lockers. "It was," I said. "She's a total natural on camera."

"Well, aren't you two BFFs again?" answered Kate. "In fact, Sophie also mentioned that you asked her to join your sleepover tomorrow night. Maybe I should come too, and we can plan your Day in the Life video?"

Fat chance — it was going to be hard enough getting the girls to allow Sophie to come, let alone Kate. Plus, Sophie had really invited herself, but I just couldn't say no. "Maybe, but I'd have to ask my mom," I said carefully, trying to buy more time. "In any case, I'm sure there'll be no shortage of fun ideas for the video!"

"Well, why don't you at least sit with us at lunch today and we'll brainstorm?" she asked. "I'm off to homeroom, but see you later!" She sashayed down the hallway without waiting for my answer.

Not to be mean, but Kate was not the type of person I would choose as a BFF. I wasn't really sure why Sophie was all about her. Then again, Sophie put the Soph in sophisticated, so it wasn't surprising that she hung out with the older girls. I just wasn't sure if I really wanted to do the same, especially when it seemed like they only cared about being in my Day in the Life video.

They didn't give me much of a choice later that day in the caf, though. "Get your booty over here, Magstar," yelled Sophie. "We've got work to do!"

I guessed it wouldn't hurt to sit with them for a few minutes. I sent an apologetic shrug toward Delaney, Willow, and Maren, who were watching with curiosity from our usual place as I headed over to Kate's table.

Sophie held out her plate as I took a seat next to her. "Carrot stick?" she offered. I shook my head no. My stomach was feeling a little rumbly, and I felt really tired all of a sudden.

"Love your outfit, Ashley," said Kate's friend, Samantha. That perked me up a little bit. I'd spent a long time picking out the right top to wear with my new skinny jeans. After all, I had to make up for Monday's fashion flub!

Kate slid her iPad across the table toward me. "Speaking of outfits, we've already mapped out pretty much your whole Day in the Life video," she said. "We know you're super busy, so we figured we'd do the legwork for you! Check it out."

They'd made a long list of ideas, like "Visit the Chanel store in downtown Portland," "Get facials at Eco-Spa," "Take viewers on a shopping tour of Main Street," and "Sleepover at Kate's." All of the ideas sounded like things I would love to do, and they added up to a pretty glamorous day! The one problem? Everything starred Kate and her friends. There was no mention of the Sleepover Girls in sight.

"These are all *a-mah-zing*," I told them. "But really, my life isn't all that glamorous. I pretty much just hang out with my best friends and my brothers and obsess over clothes online. Oh, and go to the mall a lot."

"True," said Sophie. "But fashion is all about appearances, right? So sometimes you have to gloss things over a little bit and make things seem more glam than they really are."

She had a point. We started brainstorming like mad, and before I knew it, the bell rang! I had totally lost track of the time. So much for sitting with the Sleepover Girls — Willow, Delaney, and Maren were long gone. As I gathered up my stuff for my next class, Kate put her hand on my arm. "Don't forget to ask your mom about me sleeping over," she said.

I decided to be honest. "I'm pretty sure it won't work out," I told her. "But maybe we could do something on Saturday instead?" It felt weird making plans with Kate, but I didn't want to totally blow her off.

She gave me a satisfied smile. "I'm in," she said. By the sound of it, Saturday was going to be one interesting "day in the life!"

chapter Seven

T.G.I.F. — finally! Or, as Willow, Maren, Delaney, and I thought of it, T.G.I.S.D. (Thank Goodness It's Sleepover Day!) Fridays always meant sleepovers, and tonight was my turn to host, which was super exciting. The not-so-exciting part? I still had to break the news to the girls that Sophie had invited herself to join us, and I hadn't had the heart to turn her down. Gulp.

Before school, I bought a round of strawberry-banana smoothies, hoping that might help smooth things over. After all, Delaney was still sour on Sophie after the cyberbullying disaster, and Maren had never really been a big fan of hers in the first place. My only hope was that Willow, ever the peacemaker, could help them forgive my friend and move on.

I'd texted everyone to meet me at my locker before homeroom, and sure enough, the Sleepover Girls were waiting when I arrived with smoothies in hand. "You're late," said Maren, who was rarely on time herself. "Hanging with Kate and her crew again?"

"Very funny," I said. "Consider these smoothies a peace offering?" Things weren't off to the best start.

"I bet Ash was busy counting all of the crazy votes she's getting," piped in Delaney, looking up from her phone. "It's up to almost thirty thousand now — you're practically viral! I wonder where the big spike came from."

Maybe this could be a good transition. "Well, I posted my first Stepz Shoes video last night," I told them. "Sophie helped me make it the other day, and it turned out awesome! I think Stepz tweeted a link to the contest or something. They have tons of followers, so maybe they're all voting."

Willow smiled and took a sip of her smoothie. (Healthy drinks were right up her alley!) "That is amazing, Ash," she said. "I think you have a really good shot at winning this contest."

Maren and Delaney weren't as pumped. "Since when is Sophie helping you make videos again?" asked Maren. She never missed a beat.

I took a deep breath. "Well, she's been really supportive of Magstar, and it's not like I can ignore her forever," I said, hoping they'd see my side of things. "We all make mistakes, right? I don't think that means you need to cut someone out of your life for good."

Delaney folded her arms. "Anyone who is capable of being that mean isn't a friend of mine," she said. "After everything she put Marcie through, I would think you'd feel the same."

Delaney definitely had a point. Sophie had made a fake Twitter account for Marcie and done lots of other mean things. However, she'd also been suspended for a week and said she was sorry to everyone involved. It seemed like she was willing to turn over a new leaf, so why not forgive and forget?

"Well, put yourself in her shoes," I said. "She was the new girl in town, trying to get in good with Kate Homan. It's easy to lose track of who you really are when you're trying to fit in with the popular, older girls."

"You would know," muttered Maren. But after I shot her a look, she backed down.

"Kidding, kidding," she added. Despite my great speech, Delaney didn't seem convinced, either.

It was now or never. "So I guess this probably isn't the best time to tell you that I told Sophie she could join our sleepover tonight?" I asked.

Willow spoke up first. "It's fine with me if she comes," she said, twirling her long blond hair around her finger. Grudges weren't her thing. "The more the merrier."

I turned my attention to Maren and Delaney. "Pretty please?" I asked. "It's just for one sleepover. But I understand if you're not down with it. It's not decided until all the Sleepover Girls say it is."

Maren fiddled with her smoothie straw. "I guess we can try and see how it goes," she said.

Delaney broke down, too. "Well, I won't be the lone holdout," she said. "I'm sure I can make nice, as long as she plays nice, too."

"Not a problem," I assured her, relieved. I was going to do everything in my power to ensure that there wouldn't be any problems. I'd already put together a full itinerary of fun activities, which would hopefully keep us busy enough to avoid any drama. It would be a night to remember, for sure!

That night, Delaney arrived first with her giant duffel. She was still wearing her soccer uniform from practice, and her hair was adorably tousled. "I'm starving!" she said, throwing her bag onto the sofa. "Is there anything in the fridge?"

Now that was a silly question. At my house, the kitchen was definitely the star of the show (even more than our "fun room" basement!). With our Italian family, having an empty fridge was out of the question. "Don't let my mom hear you say that," I joked. "We've got enough leftovers to feed an army!"

Delaney grinned and clapped her hands together. "Excellent," she said. "Don't mind if I do!"

She had just finished microwaving some leftover chicken parmesan when Willow and Maren showed up together. "Hola, chicas!" said Maren, shimmying her way into the kitchen. "What smells so good?"

"Oh, just a little slice of heaven, that's all," said Delaney, offering her a forkful.

Maren took a second to savor the bite. "I've said it before and I'll say it again," she said. "Mrs. Maggio definitely needs her own Food Network show. And then she can introduce me to all the fabulous TV executives." It was no secret that Maren hoped to be a famous actress one day.

Delaney offered a bite to Willow, who shook her head politely. "Oh, duh, sorry — I forgot you don't do meat," said Delaney. "Oh well. More for me!"

"What time is Sophie getting here?" asked Maren, eyeing the cupcake decorating kit I had out on the counter. "I'm getting hungry again!"

Matt chimed in from his perch at the kitchen table, where he'd been eavesdropping. "Yeah, when *is* Sophie getting here?" It was no secret that he had a crush on Sophie.

Before I could tell him to buzz off, Sophie came waltzing through the back door. "Sorry I'm late!" she said. She was dressed in a black velour jumpsuit with purple trim. "Trina got stuck working late, so it threw off my mom's timing for the whole day. Did I miss anything good?" Sophie's older sister Trina worked at a stable, so she was often at the mercy of her unpredictable work schedule.

"Nope!" I said. "We were just waiting for Matt to finish eating his dinner so we can set up the table for cupcake decorating. Ahem." I gave him a look so he would take the hint.

He threw his hands up and grabbed his plate to take it into the living room. "Five to one, I get it — I'm outnumbered," he said. "Kitchen's all yours."

I smiled as Matt walked by. "Glad you recognize our collective girl power."

chapter Eight

Now that we had the kitchen all to ourselves, I grabbed the cupcake decorating kit and danced around with it.

"Who's ready for something sweet?" I asked in a sing-song voice. "I know I am."

Coco barked and hopped up and down excitedly, as if to say she was, too. Coco really seemed to understand what was important in life — friends, food, and fun.

"I don't know," said Sophie. "The frosting might bring back bad memories of Wednesday's science class. Ashley and I came this close to getting detention, thanks to Grant Thompson!"

I noticed Delaney bristle at the mention of science class and decided to change the subject. "Speaking of Grant, I'm debating whether to send him a V-Gram next week for Valentine's Day," I said. "What do you think?"

V-Grams were these super cute Valentine cards that you could buy and send at school. They were a fund-raiser for our school council and always made a lot of money.

Willow looked impressed. "I give you credit," she said. "I could never even think about doing something like that!"

Willow was definitely the shy one of the group, even though she had a big crush on Jacob, her twin Winston's friend. Unfortunately, Jacob liked me, so it was a little bit of an awkward subject. For that very reason, we tried not to talk about it.

"Oh, c'mon, Willow," urged Sophie. "How else do you think you'll get Jacob's attention?"

I cleared my throat, hoping to change the subject again. Sophie wasn't exactly doing her best to win everyone over. I was starting to regret my decision to invite her.

"So, what about you, Maren? Do you think you and Winston will do anything for Valentine's Day?" I asked.

In one of the biggest surprises of the school year, Maren had developed a lovey-dovey relationship with Willow's twin. She'd gone from being totally grossed out by boys to the only one of us with a semi-boyfriend. A lot had changed since we started sixth grade!

Maren sniffed. She may have been all about Winston, but she didn't like calling attention to it.

"I doubt it," she said. "But if we do, I know what outfit I'll be wearing, thanks to you and the fun video shoot."

"Happy to help! Now let's make some cupcakes, shall we?" I said, laying everything out neatly on the table. My mom had already made double-chocolate cupcakes for us to decorate.

Always one to help take charge, Delaney started clearing the table and grabbed my phone. She glanced at the home screen and let out a little whoop. "Dang, girl, you have hundreds of new notifications!" she said. "You are one popular girl."

And that was the story of my life — my phone was constantly buzzing with Instagram notifications, Twitter updates, and Facebook comments, as well as emails updating me on blog comments. And I loved every second of it! I really was one lucky girl!

"Let me see," I said, grabbing it from her. There were lots of people posting pictures of their Valentine's Day outfits with the hashtag *#looksweheart* in response to my video. And the Stepz Shoes video was getting lots of comments!

So far, my YouTube channel was off to a smashing start. I clicked over to my *Stylish Tween* profile page to check if I'd gotten any more votes, and sure enough, the number was rising!

"I'm up to forty-eight thousand!" I said, excitedly showing the girls my phone. "Maybe I'll be one of the top five finalists after all."

Willow giggled. "Looks like you're neck-and-neck with a blogger named Anna Wintour's Evil Stepdaughter," she said. "I think you can take her."

"Are you kidding me?" said Sophie. "Ashley's got this in the bag. We can all keep bugging everyone we know to vote, and I'll definitely do my part. After all, it's about time I used my Twitter powers for good." She grinned slyly.

Even Delaney had to smile at that one. "You know you can count on all of us to stuff the virtual ballot box," she told me as she tore open a bag of sprinkles and began pouring them into a bowl. "Tell Anna Wintour's stepdaughter to make way for the Magstar!"

"Seriously, Ash, you are a complete and total rock star," said Maren. "Save me a seat in the front row one day at your Fashion Week runway show, 'kay?"

"You know it!" I told her. A girl could dream. "You guys can all be models in my first big show."

Sophie sucked in her cheeks and started strutting through the kitchen like she was a model. We all giggled, and then Delaney filled Sophie in on the time when we all starred in the Valley View Animal Rescue's fashion show. "That was the day my parents surprised me and we got to adopt my adorable dog, Frisco," she concluded with a big grin. "It was the best day of my life!"

I hugged Coco a little closer at the memory. "Oh yes, and I wore a Chia Pet-inspired dress. Now *that* you should have seen," I told Sophie. "Turns out moss green isn't my best color."

I poured the conversation hearts into a bowl and handed Willow a frosting pen. "Okay, now let's get this cupcake party started!"

Willow picked up one of the conversation hearts and held it up. "This one was made just for you, Ash." She laughed. "It says, 'Tweet Me!'" I giggled and took a picture of it with my phone. It would make a good Insta post later.

Never one to be outdone, Maren chimed in. "I've got an even better one: 'Be My Tweet-heart!'"

Sophie laughed right along with everyone else. "It feels good to be hanging out with you guys again," she said, scooping up Coco onto her lap. "Thanks for letting me crash your slumber party."

"You know it," I told her, putting a giant dollop of white frosting on my cupcake. "We've got a pillow with your name on it anytime you want to join us."

Delaney grinned, putting the finishing touches on her own cupcake. "Well, if Ashley wins the contest, you can come to the sleepover when we do Ashley's Day in the Life video," she offered. I gave her a grateful smile.

"Sure," said Sophie. "Ash promised me, Kate, and the girls we could all be in the video, too, so maybe we can all come!"

Delaney's face fell. "Maybe," she said, pretending to be extremely interested in her cupcake all of a sudden.

Uh-oh. I had to squash any tension before the sleepover started to go south. "Girls, I haven't even won this thing yet," I told them. "Let's focus on the present and the delicious cupcakes."

"Cupcakes really are the best," said Willow, smiling as she showed off her beautifully decorated cupcake. Then she took a huge bite, which had us all laughing again.

chapter Nine

Luckily, the rest of the sleepover went great. We played some pinball, did crazy hairstyles on each other, and even managed to get a little sleep. Sure, there'd been a few awkward moments, but overall everyone had gotten along well. I should have known it was too good to be true.

The trouble started when everyone was getting ready to leave in the morning. "Hey, Ash, want to take Frisco and Coco to the dog park in a little bit?" asked Delaney. She knew

I loved dressing Coco up in her sweater and going to the park.

Sophie spoke up before I could respond. "Actually, my mom's picking us up soon and we're going over to Kate's," she told her. I'd been hoping that little tidbit wouldn't slip out, but so much for that!

Seeing Delaney's face, I scrambled to make it better. "It's no big deal," I assured her. "Doesn't Kate live in your neighborhood? I'll just come by after and we can go to the park then; I'll text you."

Delaney shrugged. "Okay, sure," she said, managing a small smile. Maren just raised her eyebrows and kept packing her overnight bag.

The girls finished gathering their things and left quietly. So *not* how I wanted our sleepover to end. I tried to shake it off once Sophie and I were on our way to Kate's. I was already feeling a little nervous about hanging out with Kate, and I definitely didn't want my friends mad at me.

I was still trying to calm my nerves when Kate opened the door for Sophie and me. Kate was dressed in a beautiful flowy navy tunic and pinstriped leggings. (Say what you will about the girl, but her wardrobe was always on point!) "Morning," she said, standing aside to let us in. "You're just in time for omelets and crepes!"

"*Tres chic*," giggled Sophie, giving Kate a double air kiss as a hello.

When we walked into the kitchen, Samantha was already seated at the table. I hadn't known she was going to be here, too! I was definitely out of my comfort zone, but at least Sophie was with me. *She* certainly felt right at home hanging with the older girls, so I'd just follow her lead.

"Hey," said Samantha, motioning for us to sit down. "Help yourself to some of Mrs. Homan's food! This is totally yum."

If there was one thing I could find common ground with them on, it was delicious food.

But it was hard to imagine Mrs. Homan's food even coming close to my mom's! "If you insist," I said jokingly, spooning a chocolate crepe onto my plate.

Once we were all digging in, Samantha slid a stack of papers over to us. "Check this out! I'm on the yearbook committee, and I managed to sneak an early draft out of the office so you guys could see."

Kate snatched it up to take a look. "I'm sure you only picked the best pictures of us, right?" she asked, rifling through the pages.

"You know it," said Samantha. She let out a little giggle. "Unfortunately, the same can't be said for *certain* people. The photo of the girls' volleyball team is a little, ahem, unfortunate."

She flipped to the page to show us, and Kate and Sophie immediately dissolved into giggles. Kate grabbed the yearbook and pointed to the picture of Autumn Massey, one of the seventh graders.

"Talk about unfortunate!" she said. "Ashley, she looks like she could have used your styling skills on picture day."

I didn't know what to say — I'd barely been there ten minutes, and already they were living up to their mean-girl reputation. Sophie must have sensed that I felt weird, because she decided to change the subject. "You haven't even *seen* Ashley's styling skills until you see the video we did the other day," she told them, pulling out her phone.

Samantha and Kate crowded around her phone to check it out. "Wow, so Stepz gave you all of those shoes for free?" asked Kate. "You lucky duck! Some of those styles haven't even been released yet."

I softened a little. Gossiping and being mean wasn't my thing, but talking fashion definitely was. "I know, right?" I said. "The blog is a lot of work, but it's so worth it. Wanna see another Magstar video?"

At their nods, I cued up the Looks We Heart video I'd made with the girls for V-Day, and pretty soon we were scrolling through all my old videos. The girls couldn't seem to get enough! Kate even showed me a few videos from her fave fashion bloggers, some of whom I hadn't heard of before.

"These videos are awesome, Ashley," said Samantha, who seemed to follow whatever Kate said or thought. "I can't wait to help you make your Day in the Life video."

Kate's eyes lit up. "Hey! I have an idea," she said. "Why don't we walk up to Main Street and check out some of the boutiques? We can map out the places that would be good to include in Ashley's video." Main Street was one of the cutest areas in our tiny town of Valley View.

I was game. After all, I did have to turn in my sample itinerary in a few days, and they had some great ideas! "Sounds like a plan," I told her. "But first, anyone want some cupcakes?" I'd brought the leftover cupcakes from last night, figuring they could help break the ice. (Who didn't love chocolate?)

Not surprisingly, they all started digging in. "Wow — baker, fashionista, what *don't* you do?" joked Kate. "Sophie, why have you been keeping Ashley a secret from us for so long?"

I smiled. Even if I wasn't totally sure about Kate, it felt pretty good to have the coolest girl in seventh grade thinking that I was the awesome one. The lovefest continued on Main Street, where we took the shops by storm. It felt good to shop with Sophie again; while I loved shopping with the Sleepover Girls, they definitely weren't as gung ho as my fashionable friend!

The afternoon flew by as we went into one store after another. We were on our way out of Shoe Fly when I spotted three familiar faces walking down the street. It was Delaney, Maren, and Willow . . . with Delaney's dog, Frisco! And with the exception of the always happy-go-lucky Frisco, none of them looked too thrilled.

"Guess we know how you spent *your* afternoon . . . and it wasn't at the dog park with me," said Delaney with a frown.

Sensing the tension, Samantha, Kate, and Sophie decided to move along and avoid all the awkwardness.

"Hey, let's head into Sew & Tell," said Samantha. "Meet us in there, Ashley. Loved the cupcakes you guys made, by the way!" They headed into the next store, leaving me to face my friends.

I felt terrible. I'd totally forgotten to text Delaney — and about our plans to go to the dog park. "Okay, I feel awful. Am I in the doghouse now?" I asked, trying to make a joke. When they didn't respond, I made another attempt to get the conversation going. "Did I miss anything good at the park?"

Maren narrowed her eyes. "Probably nothing, compared to a shopping spree with the seventh graders," she said. I could tell she was trying to say it like a joke, but her voice didn't really sound like she was kidding.

"Yeah, when we said it was cool to start hanging out with Sophie, we didn't realize that also meant joining the queen bee and her hive," said Delaney, avoiding my eyes.

"Oh, and don't worry, we didn't want any of the leftover cupcakes we decorated anyway," said Maren, no longer able to hide the fact that she was upset. "See you later, Ash."

And they all started walking down the street together, even Willow. Planning this Day in the Life video was turning out to be much trickier than expected! And without my true co-stars, it didn't really mean a thing.

chapter Ten

I tossed and turned that night, alternately wishing I'd win the contest and worrying about making everyone happy. Kate had called to see if I wanted to hang out again on Sunday, but I hadn't responded yet. I'd tried calling Delaney, Maren, and Willow a few times, but none of them had picked up. Did they actually think I would sell them out for the seventh graders? Not in a million years.

I sprung out of bed. I knew exactly what I wanted to do. I sat down at my vanity and flipped my laptop open, typing furiously. The words flew out of me as I typed out my perfect day in the life — one that actually resembled my real life. It went a little something like this: morning primp session with a DIY mani, long bike ride with my besties, a shopping spree at the mall, pasta dinner with my family, and of course, the sleepover to end all sleepovers. Noticeably absent? Kate and her gang! And when I pressed the "send" button off to *Stylish Tween*, it felt pretty darn good.

Monday morning, I woke up feeling a lot more like myself. I flat-ironed my hair and threw on my favorite green sweater with some cute jeans and dangly earrings. Then, I printed out several copies of my Day in the Life itinerary on pink paper. By the time Gino peeked his head in the door to see if I was ready, I was raring to go. "Let's do it!" I said, bouncing off the bed.

"Well, aren't you peppy this morning?" said Gino, not sure how to take my sudden enthusiasm.

When I got to school, I saw a student council table set up in the front entrance. Sloane Stevens and Tyler Mathews were selling V-Grams! I approached them excitedly.

"I'll take three, please," I said, filling out the cards to my three favorite people. Grant was the furthest thing from my mind right now. "Oh, and can you put these inside the envelopes, too?" I neatly folded the Day in the Life itineraries and handed them over with the completed V-Grams.

By the time lunch came around, I was hoping my besties had gotten their V-Grams. I couldn't handle the idea of another day going by with them being mad! I approached our table tentatively, when Delaney burst into a big grin. "Well, if it isn't the Valentine's Fairy," she said with a smile. "Thanks for the mail."

I let out a sigh of relief and sat down with the paper bag lunch I'd packed. "Whew!" I said. "For a minute there, I thought my 'Tweet-hearts' didn't want me around anymore."

"Sorry about that," said Maren. "I guess we overreacted yesterday. It just felt really weird to see you being so buddy-buddy with the royal court."

Delaney decided to weigh in. "Yeah, and I was kind of hurt, being that we've been behind you every step of the way," she said. "But I know you would never really leave us in the dust."

I took a bite of my caprese sandwich. "Totally understandable," I said. "And for a minute, they did suck me in. I'll admit it. But any day in the life without you guys isn't worth living!"

When I really took a second to think about it, the whole thing felt like déjà vu. After all, when Sophie had first moved here, I'd kind of fallen under her spell, too. At her suggestion, I'd totally changed my look to be less colorful and more sophisticated (read: all black). The girls hadn't been big fans of Sophie — or my sudden makeover — but they'd helped me find my groove again. (Sense a theme here?)

Willow smiled. "I think your itinerary turned out perfect," she told me, her face turning hot red all of a sudden. She lowered her voice. "Ummm, Grant and Jacob are coming over to our table."

My heart skipped a beat. Did my hair look okay? I felt a tap on my shoulder. "Hey, Ashley," said Grant. "Instead of sending you a V-Gram, I thought you might appreciate this."

He set a plate down in front of me that had four graham crackers, each with a word written on it in frosting. Together they spelled out, "Happy Valentine's Day, Ashley." I absolutely melted! This was way better than any V-Gram.

I gave him a smile and took a little bite. "Tastes way better than an edible plant cell, especially when you're not throwing it at me!" I joked. "See you in science class."

He and Jacob headed off, and Delaney, Willow, and Maren all let out a collective squeal.

"Did that just happen?" asked Delaney.

I was asking myself the same question. Maybe my crush was a two-way street after all? I whipped out my phone so I could grab a pic of my favorite V-day gift ever. Except I wasn't going to post this one — I was going to keep it all for myself.

Maren nudged me. "Don't look now, but we have another visitor," she said. I looked over my shoulder to see Kate confidently walking over to our table.

"Hey, Ashley! I never heard back from you about hanging out yesterday," she said. "Want to get together after school and finalize your list? The deadline is this Wednesday, after all," she said, smiling big.

I smiled brightly and whipped out my pink sheet of paper. "Actually, it's all dunzo!" I told her, handing the paper over. "Thanks for offering to help, though."

Kate gave it a quick scan. "I see you didn't include any of my ideas," she muttered, her face turning dark. "Too bad. I would think you'd have wanted some fellow fashionistas in the video with you!" She gave Maren, Delaney, and Willow a disapproving glance.

I tried to be diplomatic. "It was so sweet of you guys to try to help, but I have to keep it real with my readers," I told her. "These three are the stylish tweens who co-star in my everyday life!"

"Well, good luck with it, then," said Kate in an insincere voice. "I've been thinking about starting a fashion blog of my own, anyway." She headed off toward her table without saying goodbye.

So much for us starting a friendship — I guess she'd only been laying it on thick to be part of the video.

Maren tried to lighten the mood. "Wait, is *she* Anna Wintour's evil stepdaughter?" she asked, prompting a laugh from all of us.

"Who knows?" I told her. What Kate thought didn't really matter to me, and honestly, it didn't even matter to me whether I won the contest. (Well, maybe a little bit.) All that mattered was fashion, fun, and — of course — friendship! My three besties were the ones who helped my Magstar shine bright, and that meant more than any red carpet ever could.

The Friendship Quiz

Do your friendships last through thick and thin?
Or do you get going when the going gets tough?
Take this quiz to learn more about yourself
and your relationships.

1. You win tickets to an awesome sold-out concert!
   It's on the same night as your BFF's b-day, and she
   wants to throw a beach bonfire. What do you do?

   a) See if your friend wants to join you for the
      concert instead. (2)

   b) Sorry, but when the front row calls, you've
      got to answer! You'll make it up to her with
      a killer gift. (1)

   c) Give the tickets to your sibling and attend
      the party. Nothing comes between you and
      your BFF. (3)

2. A pretty crazy rumor is going around about a
   close friend. You overhear someone say, "I don't
   know who'll hang out with him anymore." You:

a) Slowly distance yourself from your friend, hoping no one will think the same about you. (1)

b) Tell your friend so he has a chance to put an end to the rumor. (2)

c) Talk to the person spreading the rumor, and set the record straight. Friends will always stick up for each other. (3)

3. Your friend is hesitant to go to the fall dance because she's afraid of looking silly on the dance floor. What's your reaction?

a) You wanted to go, but you agree to stay home with her. (3)

b) You encourage your friend to go. You'll hit the dance floor together. (2)

c) She's being a baby. She can stay home, but you're going to go anyway. (1)

4. Your friend wants to skip cheer practice and go shopping. She asks you to lie to the coach for her. What would you do?

a) Happen to "slip" and say where your friend is in front of your coach. It's not fair that she gets to have all the fun! (1)

b) Cover for her with the coach. After all, she'd do the same for you. (3)

c) Say "no thanks." She'll have to talk to the coach on her own. (2)

5. It's your turn to walk the dog after school, but you get invited to a popular girl's home after school. You:

   a) Beg your brother to do doggie duty just this once. (1)

   b) Turn down the invite and walk your four-legged friend but pout the rest of the day. (3)

   c) Figure out a way to do both. You can't leave your puppy hanging! (2)

6. When you make a promise, it means:

   a) You've got my word — unless my fingers are crossed! (1)

   b) I'll plan to do what I say, but if anything changes, I'll let you know. (2)

   c) The deal is sealed forever! (3)

7. You've gone on a two-week family vacation. When you return, you hear that your best friend has been talking about you behind your back. You:

   a) Have an honest chat with your friend. Let her know that her behavior hurt, but you're willing to give her another chance. (2)

b) Do the same to her. Now she'll know what it feels like. (1)

c) Forget it ever happened. You don't want to risk losing her friendship. (3)

8. At a sleepover, the girls start pressuring you to spill another friend's secret. What do you do?

   a) Stress out and go home. You can't blab, but you don't want to disappoint your other friends either. (3)

   b) Tell them "no way!" A true friend never spills secrets. (2)

   c) Spill the beans, but make them swear it never leaves the room. (1)

9. Your BFF from elementary school is moving back to town, but you now have a new best friend. You feel:

   a) Annoyed. You hope she doesn't bring up little-kid stuff in front of your new BFF. (1)

   b) Excited. You can't wait to reconnect with your old friend. (2)

   c) Guilty. You hope she doesn't get upset with you for moving on. (3)

10. What's your relationship with your best friend like?

a) I can totally count on her and vice versa. (2)

b) Which one? It's an ever-rotating cast of characters. (1)

c) We're attached at the hip! No one understands me like she does. (3)

11. Your little sister accidentally breaks your mom's favorite vase. What do you tell her?

a) "Stinks to be you right now!" (1)

b) "I'll tell her I knocked it over. I don't want you to get in trouble." (3)

c) "Let's go talk to Mom right now. She'll understand it was just an accident." (2)

12. What do your friends love most about you?

a) Your generosity (3)

b) Your spontaneous nature (1)

c) Your loyalty (2)

13. You and your BFF have been in drama club together forever. This year you want to join the soccer team instead, but now your friend is mad. How do you deal?

a) Tell her she's being a big baby and start hanging out with girls from the soccer team. (1)

b) Try to talk it out. Explain your choice, and reassure her that no sport could ever replace your friendship. (2)

c) Stay in the drama club to avoid losing your friend. (3)

14. You're shopping with your cousin when she asks you to lend her money for a new handbag. You:

a) Say "no way!" You might find something you really want to spend it on. (1)

b) Offer to lend her the money, under the condition that she'll pay you back tomorrow. (2)

c) Cough up the cash without thinking twice. You call it an early birthday gift. (3)

15. Your friends come over for a movie night. You had your heart set on watching the latest movie musical. Your friends are into the new zombie flick. Which one do you watch?

a) Neither. If you can't watch your movie, then you won't watch anything. (1)

b) Zombies rule! A good host always sides with her guests. (3)

c) You offer a compromise. Watch the musical first, then the zombie movie. You have plenty of time for both. (2)

15 to 25 points: You are a fickle pickle! Sometimes when the going gets tough, you tend to get going. That's not a strong basis for friendship. Being a loyal friend means being able to be trusted. Good friends do what they say they're going to do. They keep your secrets and are there to support you no matter what. It may be time to give your relationship style a makeover. Otherwise your friendships may fizzle fast.

26 to 35 points: You are a forever friend! Your friends know they have a true friend in you. It's practically impossible to break the rock-solid bonds you form with your friends. And when friction does happen, you're honest and up-front. Even though you'll do almost anything for a friend, you rarely compromise your own integrity. Thanks to your steadfast loyalty, you have lots of friends you can lean on as well.

36 to 45 points: You are too true blue. The good news is you've got a huge heart. The bad news is you so badly want to please others that it could affect your own happiness! It's okay to put yourself first sometimes and still be a forever friend. In fact, your friends might even respect you more for giving that same loyalty to yourself.

Note: This text was taken from *Are You a Good Friend?* by Jen Jones (Capstone Press, 2012).

sleepover *Girls*

Willow's
SPRING BREAK
ADVENTURE

by Jen Jones

Can't get enough Sleepover Girls?
Check out the first chapter of

Willow's Spring Break Adventure

chapter One

Ahhh! I took a big whiff of the yummy-smelling rosemary oil on my wrist, hoping it would help me pay attention to the test in front of me. My mom had promised that the oil would boost my ability to focus as she'd spritzed it on me that morning. (She was hippie-dippy like that, and I loved her all the more for it.) But how was anyone supposed to focus when spring break was just a few short hours away?

It wasn't easy, that was for sure — especially since my besties and I were going to be heading to Whidbey Island. My family made the trip every year, but this was the first time I'd ever been allowed to invite anyone. Naturally, I'd invited my BFFs Ashley, Delaney, and Maren. It was going to be like one giant weeklong sleepover, and I was bursting at the seams with excitement! But first? I had to make it through midterms. (No easy task.)

With just a few minutes left of class, I buckled down to try to solve the last few pre-algebra probs. I triumphantly finished the test just as the bell started to sound.

"Woo-hoo!" I exclaimed in relief. "Oops, did I just say that out loud?"

"That you did," said Jacob Willis, striding up next to me as I gathered my stuff. "I'm pretty sure you just said what we were all feeling. So, woo-hoo right back at you!"

I tried to fight the hot blush taking over my cheeks. Jacob was my twin Winston's best friend, and for the longest time, I'd had a crush on him. But at my Halloween birthday party, I'd found out that he had a crush on my BFF Ashley. Since then, I'd been trying to see Jacob as just a friend. But much like trying to focus on math tests, it didn't always work.

I stuffed my textbook into my bag and tried to think of something witty to say. "I see I'm not the only one counting the minutes until spring break," I said, feeling a smile creep onto my face.

"Definitely not," said Jacob, as we spilled out into the hallway with the rest of the class. "I'm not sure if San Francisco is ready for me and your brother to roll in!"

How lucky was Winston to be going on spring break with Jacob and his family? (Answer: so, so lucky.) Thankfully, my consolation prize was just as good — getting to take my besties on my trip! I couldn't wait to show them all the reasons I loved gorgeous, nature-rific Whidbey Island.

The thought of Whidbey Island helped me get through the day, which seemed to drag on and on. When the bell finally signaled the end of school, mass chaos broke out. People were running through the hallways, and whoops of excitement filled the air. Somehow I managed to spot Maren in the midst of all the craziness.

"I don't know what I'm more excited for — the fact that Delaney's sleepover is tonight, or the fact that we're leaving for Whidbey on Sunday," I said with a giant smile. Spring break was finally starting! "Wanna go grab a juice to celebrate?" My parents owned a health store called Creative Juices, and it was the perfect place to nab a tasty and nutritious spring break treat!

Maren crossed her eyes and stuck out her tongue. "As tempting as a wheatgrass smoothie sounds, I've gotta go home and pack before the Little Monsters come over and tear up the place," she said. Her mom had recently gotten remarried, and her new step-sibs stayed at her house every other weekend. Needless to say, it hadn't exactly been like *The Brady Bunch* right off the bat! But she was slowly making peace with it . . . and them.

"Copy that," I told her. "Maybe you can send Alice and Ace a postcard from Whidbey Island? That would earn you big-time points with Gary."

Maren grinned. "Yeah, except most postcards say 'Wish You Were Here,' and well, I cannot tell a lie," she said in a deep George Washington voice. If her bouncy red curls were white, she probably would have looked like ol' George, too!

Before I could come up with a snappy reply, I was blinded by someone putting her hands over my eyes. "Guess who?" sang a girly voice from behind me. "I'll give you a hint. She totally finished midterms and has a hot pink suitcase that's raring to go to Whidbey Island!"

I pulled the hands off my eyes and turned around to find a very excited Ashley. Much like everyone else, she was bouncing off the walls now that spring break had begun. And I didn't blame her one bit!

"Well, well, if it isn't our very own Magstar," I said. Magstar was Ashley's super-successful fashion blog (named after her last name, Maggio). Sometimes we used it as her nickname, too.

Ashley whipped out her phone. "Oooh, that reminds me — I have to check the notifications on my latest video!" she said, eagerly scrolling through the dozens of new updates.

"Not so fast," said Maren, stealing it out of her hands. "You're on vacation, remember? I say you leave all the blog stuff behind this week and have some offline adventures!" She held the phone up high in the air so Ashley couldn't reach.

Ashley jumped up and snatched the phone back, but she put it in her jeans pocket instead of looking at it again. "I'll try, but I'm not making any promises!" she said. "I get the shakes if I'm off social media for too long."

I checked my watch. "Speaking of shakes, I've gotta get to the shop," I told them. "Can one of your moms drop me off, pretty please?"

Ashley put her arm around me. "I'm sure Gino will be happy to drive you in his weirdo-wagon," she said. Her brother's beat-up blue station wagon often got us from point A to point B (but barely).

I heaved my backpack over my shoulder as we all started heading for the exit. Most of the other students were long gone. It hadn't taken long for the hallway to clear out — this place would be a ghost town for the next week.

"Luckily, we have way more reliable transportation to Whidbey," I told her. "Though going there in the Gino-mobile would definitely add to the adventure!"

Four BEST FRIENDS plus one weekly tradition equals a whole lot of FUN!

Join in by following Delaney, Maren, Ashley, and Willow's adventures in the Sleepover Girls series. Every Friday, new memories are made as these sixth-grade girls gather together for crafts, fashion, cooking, and of course girl talk! Grab your pillow, settle in, and get to know the Sleepover Girls.

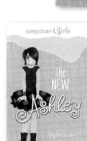

sleepover Girls

Ashley GOES VIRAL

by Jen Jones

sleepover Girls

Delaney vs. THE BULLY

by Jen Jones

sleepover Girls

DOG DAYS for *Delaney*

by Jen Jones

sleepover Girls

Maren LOVES LUKE LEWIS

by Jen Jones

sleepover Girls

Maren's NEW FAMILY

by Jen Jones

sleepover Girls

The NEW *Ashley*

by Jen Jones

sleepover Girls

Willow's BOY-CRAZY BIRTHDAY

by Jen Jones

sleepover Girls

Willow's SPRING BREAK ADVENTURE

by Jen Jones

Want to throw a sleepover party your friends will never forget?

Let the Sleepover Girls help!
The Sleepover Girls Craft titles
are filled with easy recipes, crafts,
and other how-tos combined with
step-by-step instructions and colorful
photos that will help you throw the best
sleepover party ever! Grab all eight of
the Sleepover Girls Craft titles before
your next party so you can create
unforgettable memories.

About the Author:
Jen Jones

Los Angeles-based author and
journalist Jen Jones speaks fluent
tween. She has written more than
seventy books about celebrities,
crafting, cheerleading, fashion, and
just about any other obsession a
girl in middle school could have —
including her popular *Team Cheer!* and
Sleepover Girls series for Capstone.

About the Illustrator:
Paula Franco

Paula was born and raised in Argentina, and she studied Illustration, animation, and graphic design at Instituto Superior de Comunicacion Visual in Rosario, Argentina. After graduating, Paula moved to Italy for two years to learn more about illustration. Paula now lives in Argentina and works as a full-time illustrator. Her work is published worldwide. She spends a lot of her free time wandering around bookshops and playing with her rescued dogs.